Once upon a time,

in a land where horses
were mythical beasts,
found only in the pages
of books for children,

it was common to see a unicorn.

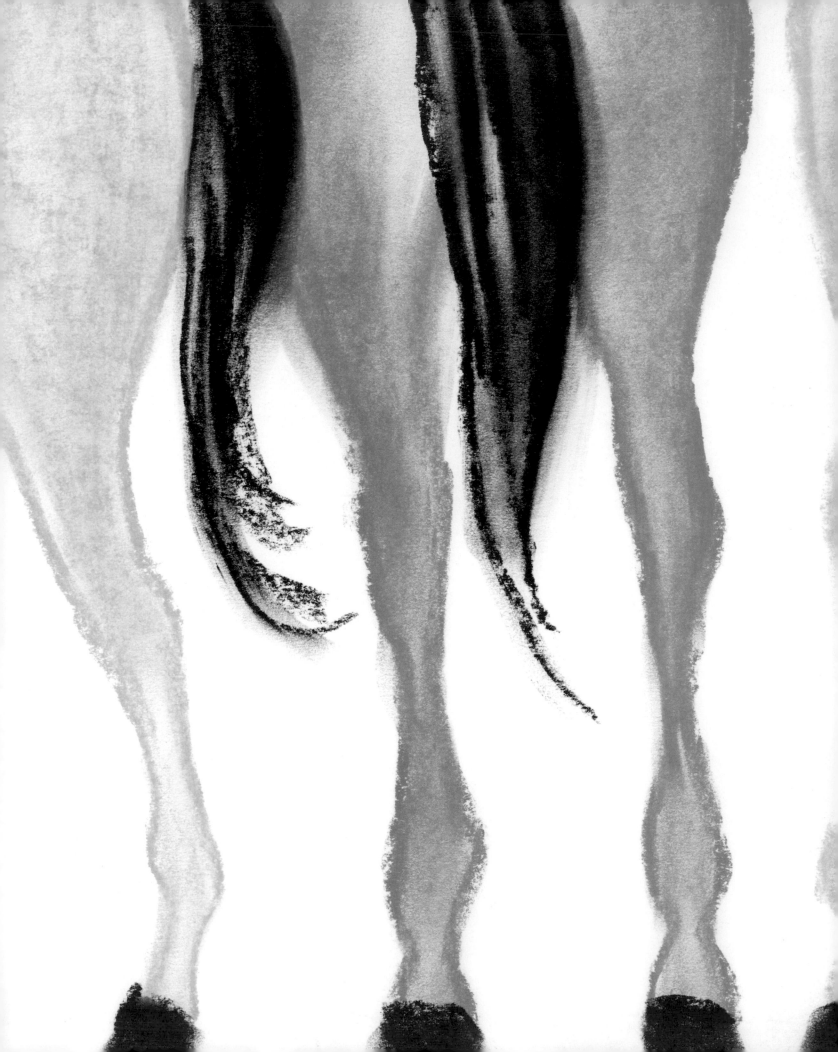

But not one
this size.

THE

Teeny-

Unic

Weeny

corn

BY SHAWN HARRIS

Alfred A. Knopf · New York

The teeny-weeny unicorn lived with
his family in a large palace.

For him, it was an extra-large palace.

The steps were
extra large.

The stoops were
extra large.

The rugs were extra large.

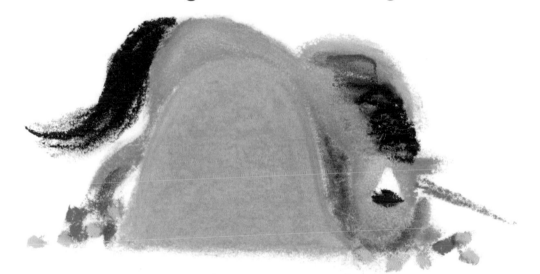

The food was extra large.

And the toys and games, too.

When the teeny-weeny unicorn's brother and sister played chess, they used him in place of the missing piece. "Can I have a turn?" he asked.

"You're too teeny-weeny," said Fancy Annie. "I'll move you when I'm ready." She moved her rook instead.

"Captured your pawn!" brayed Prince Butterscotch.

He knocked the teeny-weeny unicorn over
with the butt of his knight.

On nice days, their parents lounged on the
ramparts while the kids swam in the moat.
"Check out my splash," Fancy Annie whinnied,
and did a cannonball off the drawbridge.

"Can I have a turn?" asked the teeny-weeny unicorn.
"You're too teeny-weeny," said Prince Butterscotch.
"A gumball would make a bigger splash than you."

Fancy Annie surfaced, spitting a mouthful of moat water. "You're so teeny-weeny, you'd get lost in the lawn!"

The teeny-weeny unicorn stamped his teeny-weeny hoof.

"I'm sick and tired of being teeny-weeny!"

And into the garden he ran,
crying teeny-weeny tears.

When he tired of galloping,

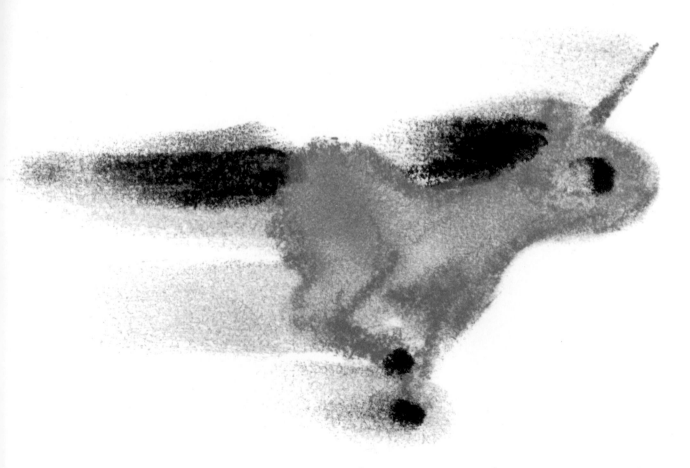

he cantered.

Then trotted.

Then walked.

"I *am* lost in the lawn,"
he admitted sadly.

Just then, a gnome came huffing and puffing through the grass.
"I've been chasing you for ages!"

"Oh," said the teeny-weeny unicorn.
"I'm sorry."
"Sorry doesn't feed the bullfrog," she said, trying to catch her breath.
The teeny-weeny unicorn was confused.
"What bullfrog?"

The gnome plucked a dandelion seed and picked her tooth with it. "I sure do pity giants like you, lumbering about, unaware of anybody but yourselves."

The teeny-weeny unicorn was extra confused.

"What giants?"

She shook her head. "Follow me."

No more than ten yards back, they came to a sporty roadster, brand-new, apart from the giant hoofprint.

The gnome pointed. "See what you've done?"
"You must be mistaken," said the teeny-weeny
unicorn. "I am *much* too teeny-weeny to smash a car."

The gnome squinted up at him. "You're huge."
"I'm not huge," said the teeny-weeny
unicorn. "You're just eeny-teeny-weeny."

"Wrong," said the gnome.
"I'm just the right size.
Now put your hoof here
and let's see
if it fits."

He was guilty.

But also
a little proud.

But mostly guilty!

"There must be some way I can repay you,"
cried the teeny-weeny unicorn.

"Two hundred fifty thousand," said the gnome.
"DOLLARS?"
The teeny-weeny unicorn whistled. "Isn't that
a lot for such a small car?"

"That's the knock on it," said the gnome.
"But she handles like a dream."
"I'll have to ask my parents . . . ,"
the teeny-weeny unicorn said
doubtfully.
The gnome climbed onto
his snout and mounted
his horn—

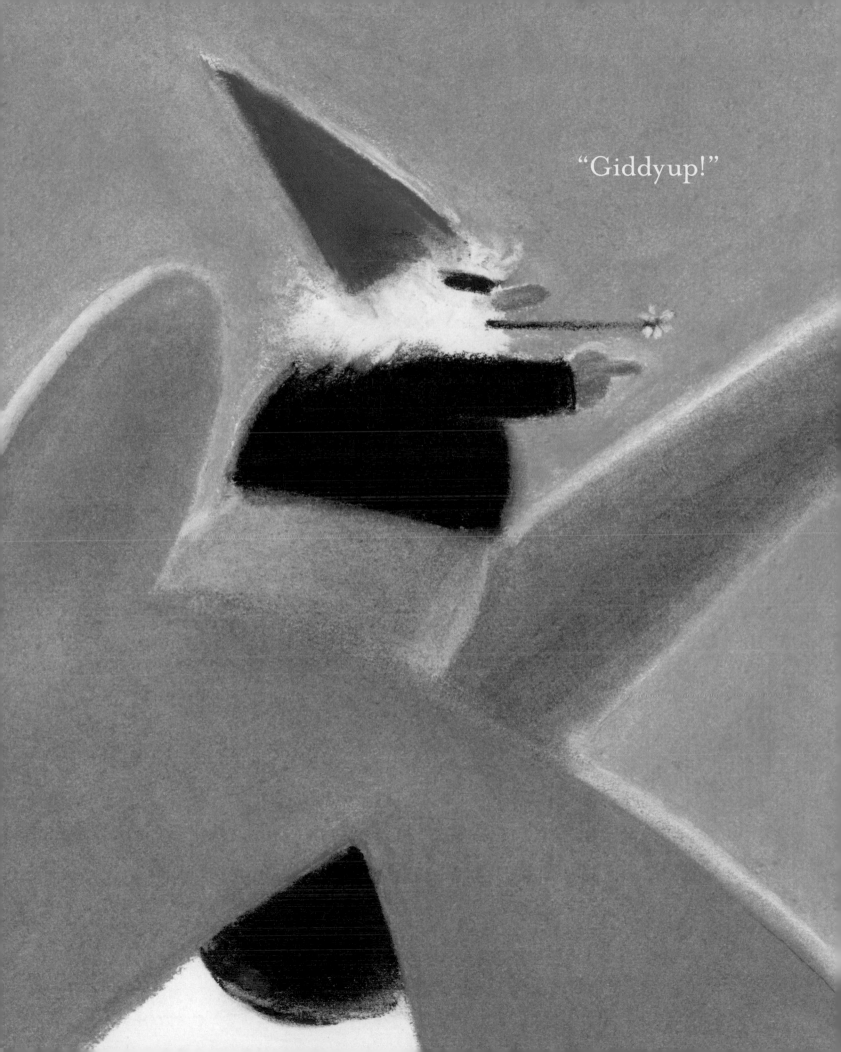

"Giddyup!"

They galloped.

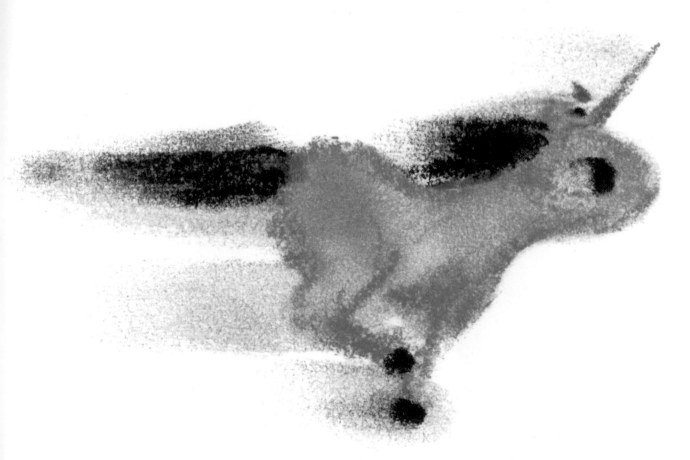

Then cantered.

Then trotted.

Then walked to the castle door.

The teeny-weeny unicorn's teeth clacked.
"Relax, kid," said the gnome. "I have a
big brother about your size. He lives under a
bridge. But if he asked, I'd give him the gold
from my molars. Know what I'm saying?"

"Sort of," said the teeny-weeny unicorn.

"Family's family," said the gnome,
and rang the bell.

She also did all the talking.

Unicorns, like most living species, have no use for money—but luckily, their palace had formerly belonged to a terrible hoarder of the stuff. The unicorns were glad to be rid of some clutter.

A carriage was piled high with gold, cash, and coins. No one even bothered counting it.

The teeny-weeny unicorn turned to Fancy Annie and Prince Butterscotch.

"I would pull the cart," he said, "but I'm too teeny-weeny."

A footman appeared.
"Your Highnesses, your harnesses."
Fancy Annie and Prince Butterscotch
grumbled with their noses in the
gravel, while many buckles and bits
were pulled snug.

"When we get back," said
Fancy Annie, "you owe us
big-time."

Prince Butterscotch shook
his mane. "You're lucky you're
our little brother."

"Family's family!" said the
gnome, taking the reins.

And off she drove them,
to wherever she lived.

The teeny-weeny unicorn *did* feel lucky to have a big brother and sister. But that didn't mean he couldn't savor the days they were gone!

Of course he played chess,

and did lots of cannonballs.

He also had a great adventure with the ghost in the north tower.

But that's a bigger story, and this book is running short on pages. So I will tell you this instead:

We are all teeny-weeny.

We are all giant.

And we are all just the right size.

The End.

For Vanessa Jo, my little sister
—Shawnie

THIS IS A BORZOI BOOK PUBLISHED BY ALFRED A. KNOPF

Copyright © 2024 by Shawn Harris

All rights reserved. Published in the United States by Alfred A. Knopf,
an imprint of Random House Children's Books, a division of Penguin Random House LLC, New York.

Knopf, Borzoi Books, and the colophon are registered trademarks of Penguin Random House LLC.

Visit us on the Web! rhcbooks.com

Educators and librarians, for a variety of teaching tools, visit us at RHTeachersLibrarians.com

Library of Congress Cataloging-in-Publication Data is available upon request.
ISBN 978-0-593-57188-0 (trade) — ISBN 978-0-593-57189-7 (lib. bdg.) — ISBN 978-0-593-57190-3 (ebook)

The text of this book is set in 23-point Mrs Eaves OT Roman.
The art was made with chalk pastels.
Edited by Rotem Moscovich
Book design by Nicole de las Heras

MANUFACTURED IN CHINA
10 9 8 7 6 5 4 3 2 1
First Edition